STAR TREK ™

THE ORIGINAL SERIES

President and Publisher
MIKE RICHARDSON

Editor
IAN TUCKER

Assistant Editor
MEGAN WALKER

Designer
SARAH TERRY

Digital Art Technician
ALLYSON HALLER

Special Thanks to John Van Citters at CBS Studios and Risa Kessler at RHK Creative Services

STAR TREK: THE ORIGINAL SERIES™ ADULT COLORING BOOK

Published by Dark Horse Books
A division of Dark Horse Comics, Inc.
10956 SE Main Street, Milwaukie, OR 97222

DarkHorse.com

To find a comics shop in your area, call the Comic Shop
Locator Service toll-free at (888) 266-4226.
International Licensing: (503) 905-2377

First edition: November 2016 | ISBN 978-1-50670-252-0

1 3 5 7 9 10 8 6 4 2
Printed in the United States of America

STAR TREK™

THE ORIGINAL SERIES

ADULT COLORING BOOK

With Illustrations by

IVÁN FERNÁNDEZ SILVA

JUAN FRIGERI

ALEJANDRO GIRALDO

GABRIEL GUZMÁN

FEDERICA MANFREDI

DARK HORSE BOOKS

Space: the final frontier.
These are the voyages of the Starship Enterprise.

Its five-year mission: to explore strange new worlds, to seek out new life and new civilizations . . .

Stardate 1313.8

"Have I ever mentioned you play an irritating game of chess, Mr. Spock?"

"Morals are for men, not gods."

Stardate 1512.2

"Captain to crew: Those of you who have served for long on this vessel have encountered alien life forms. You know the greatest danger facing us is . . . ourselves, an irrational fear of the unknown. There's no such thing as the unknown, only things temporarily hidden, temporarily not understood."

"We must drink. This is tranya. I hope you relish it as much as I."

Stardate 1672.1

"If I seem insensitive to what you're going through, Captain, understand—it's the way I am."

"I have to take him back . . . inside myself. I can't survive without him. I don't want to take him back. He's like an animal, a thoughtless, brutal animal, yet it's me . . . me."

Stardate 1513.1

"It isn't just a beast. It is
intelligent and the last of its kind."

Stardate 1704.2

"Stand! No farther. No escape for you. You'll either leave this war bloodied, or with my blood on your swords."

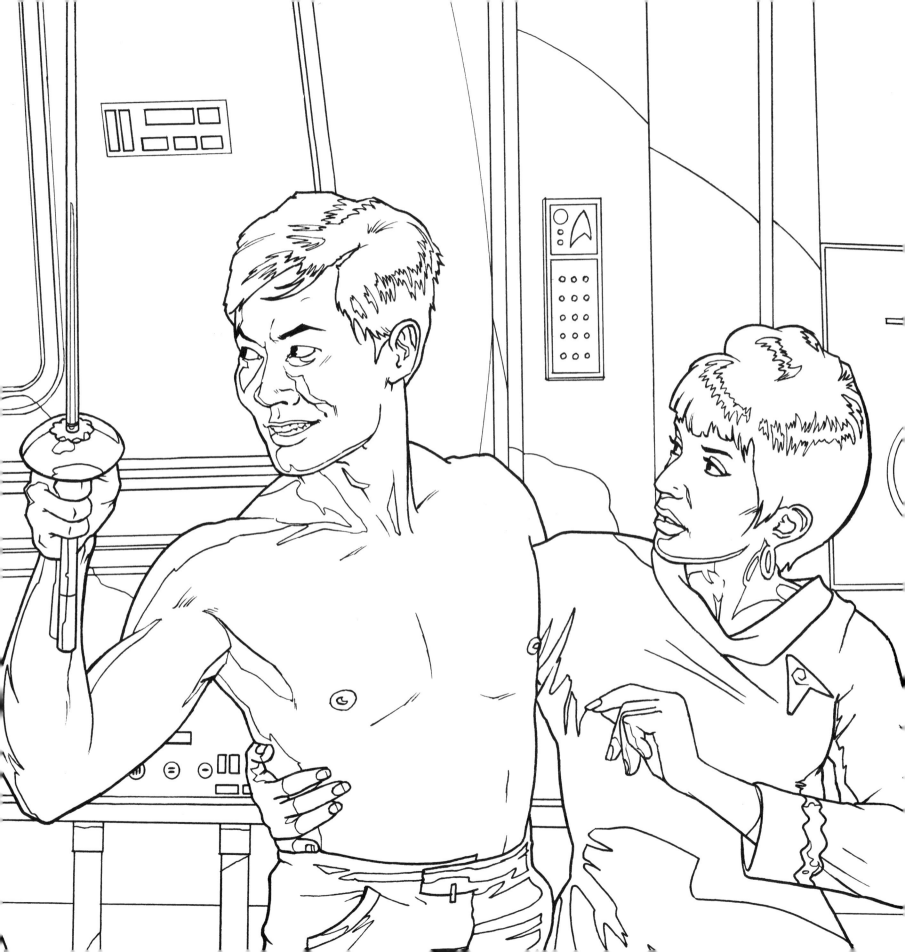

Stardate 1533.6

"Oh, on the Starship Enterprise
There's someone who's in Satan's guise,
Whose devil's ears and devil's eyes
Could rip your heart from you!
At first his look could hypnotize,
And then his touch would barbarize.
His alien love could victimize . . .
And rip your heart from you!
And that's why female astronauts
Oh, very female astronauts
Wait terrified and overwrought
To find what he will do.
Oh, girls in space, be wary, be wary, be wary!
Girls in space, be wary!
We know not what he'll do."

Stardate 1709.2

*"He did exactly what I would have done.
I won't underestimate him again."*

"As you may recall from your histories, this conflict was fought—by our standards today—with primitive atomic weapons and in primitive space vessels which allowed no quarter, no captives. Nor was there even ship-to-ship visual communication. Therefore, no human, Romulan, or ally has ever seen the other. Earth believes the Romulans to be warlike, cruel, treacherous. And only the Romulans know what they think of Earth."

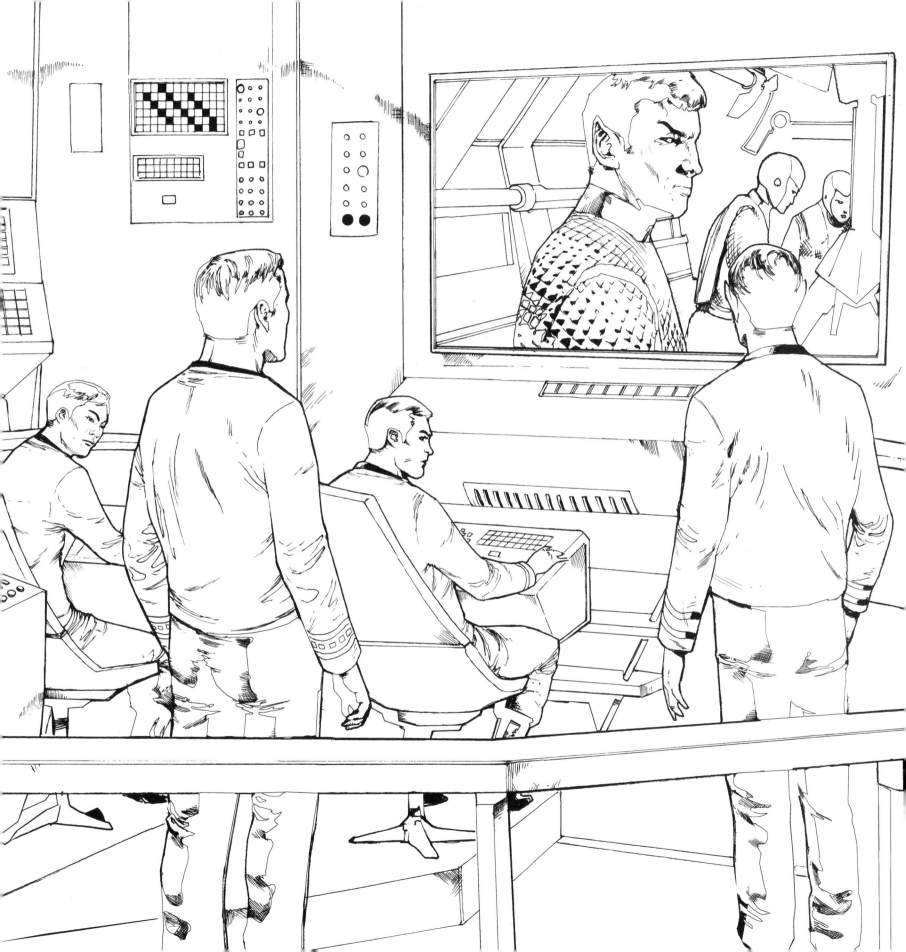

Stardate 2712.4

"In android form, a human being can have practical immortality. Can you see what I'm offering mankind?"

Stardate 2821.5

"Now, look. We may all die here. At least
let us die like men, not machines."

Stardate 2947.3

"I wouldn't want to slow the wheels of progress. But then, on the other hand, I wouldn't want those wheels to run over my client in their unbridled haste."

Stardate 3012.4

"Captain—Jim, please. Don't stop me. Don't let him stop me. It's your career and Captain Pike's life. You must see the rest of the transmission."

"His mind is as active as yours and mine but it's trapped inside a useless, vegetating body. He's kept alive mechanically—a battery-driven heart."

Stardate 3025.3

"Oh, them, well . . . I was thinking about a little cabaret I know on Rigel II, and, uh . . . there were these two girls in the chorus line. And, well, here they are! Well, after all, I am on shore leave."

Stardate 2124.5

"I want to learn all about your feelings on war and killing and conquest, that sort of thing. Do you know that you're one of the few predator species that preys even on itself?"

Stardate 3045.6

"Like most humans, I seem to have an instinctive revulsion to reptiles. I must fight to remember that this is an intelligent, highly advanced individual, the captain of a starship like myself. Undoubtedly, a dangerously clever opponent."

Stardate 3113.2

"We cannot return him to Earth, Captain. He already knows too much about us and is learning more. I do not specifically refer to Captain Christopher, but suppose an unscrupulous man were to gain certain knowledge of man's future. Such a man could manipulate key industries, stocks, and even nations, and in so doing, change what must be. And if it is changed, Captain, you and I, and all that we know, might not even exist."

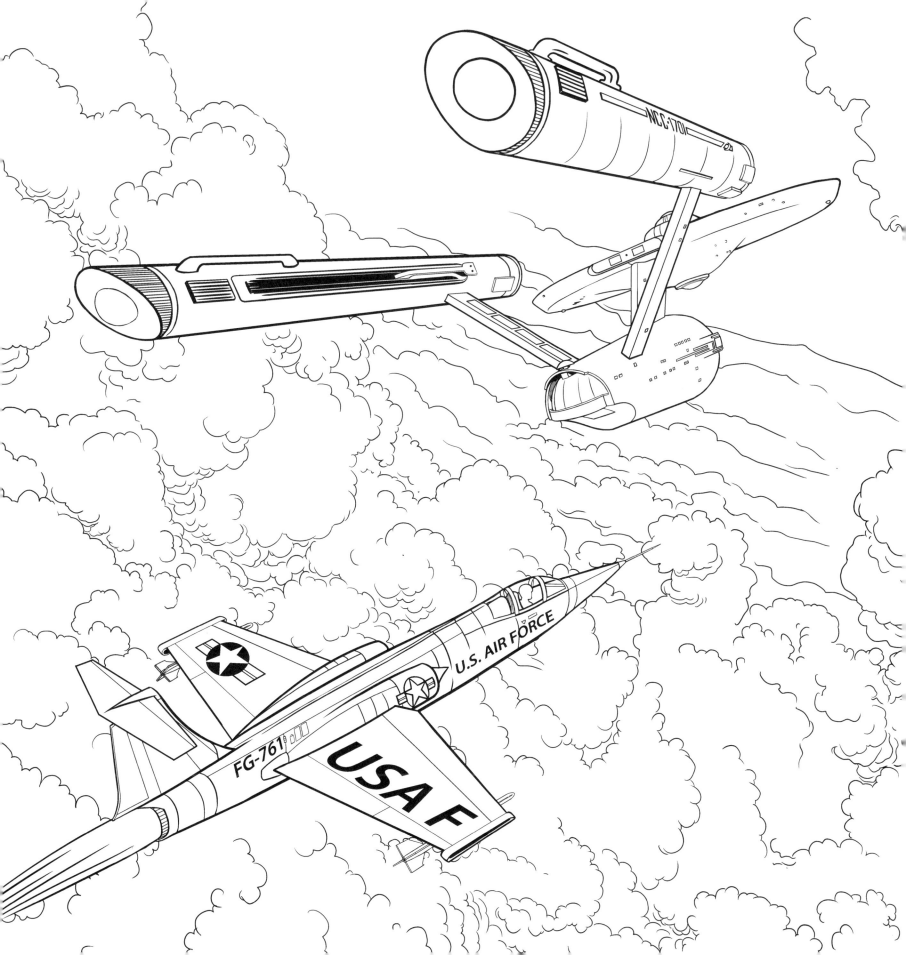

Stardate 3141.9

"Nothing ever changes, except man. Your technical accomplishments? Improve a mechanical device and you may double productivity, but improve man and you gain a thousandfold. I am such a man."

"The trip is over. The battle begins again, only this time it's not a world we win. It's a universe."

Stardate 3196.1

"The Horta has a very logical mind—
and after close association with
humans, I find that curiously refreshing."

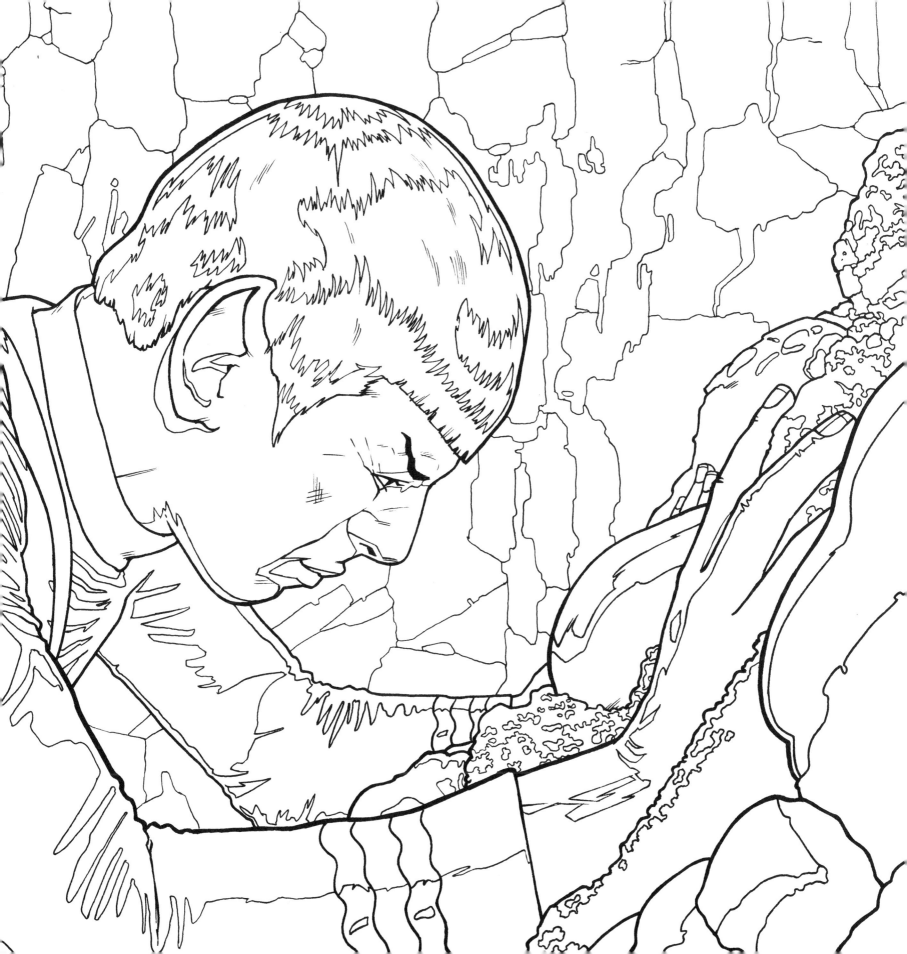

Stardate 3198.4

"You do not like to be pushed. Very good.
You may be a man I can deal with."

Stardate Unknown

"For us, time does not exist. McCoy, back somewhere in the past, has effected a change in the course of time. All Earth history has been changed. There is no Starship Enterprise. We have only one chance. We have asked the Guardian to show us Earth's history again. Spock and I will go back into time ourselves and attempt to set right whatever it was that McCoy changed."

"One day soon, man is going to be able to harness incredible energies, maybe even the atom . . . energies that could ultimately hurl us to other worlds in . . . in some sort of spaceship. And the men that reach out into space will be able to find ways to feed the hungry millions of the world and to cure their diseases. They will be able to find a way to give each man hope and a common future. And those are the days worth living for."

Stardate 3287.2

"It is not life as we know or understand
it, yet it is obviously alive. It exists."

Stardate 3018.2

"If we weren't missing two officers and a third one dead, I'd say someone was playing an elaborate trick or treat on us."

Stardate 3219.4

"I can't take her away from here. If I do, she'll die. If I leave her, she'll die of loneliness. I owe everything to her. I can't leave her. I love her."

Stardate 3497.2

"The last thing I'll want around is
a ham-handed ship's captain."

Stardate 3468.1

"All right, we're here at your invitation. Would you mind telling us what you want without all the Olympian generalities?"

Stardate 3372.7

"I burn, T'Pau. My eyes are flame. My heart is flame. Thee has the power, T'Pau. In the name of my fathers . . . forbid. Forbid!"

Stardate 4202.9

"A cranky transporter's a mighty finicky piece of machinery to be gambling your life on, sir."

"I intend to get a lot closer. I'm going to ram her right down that thing's throat."

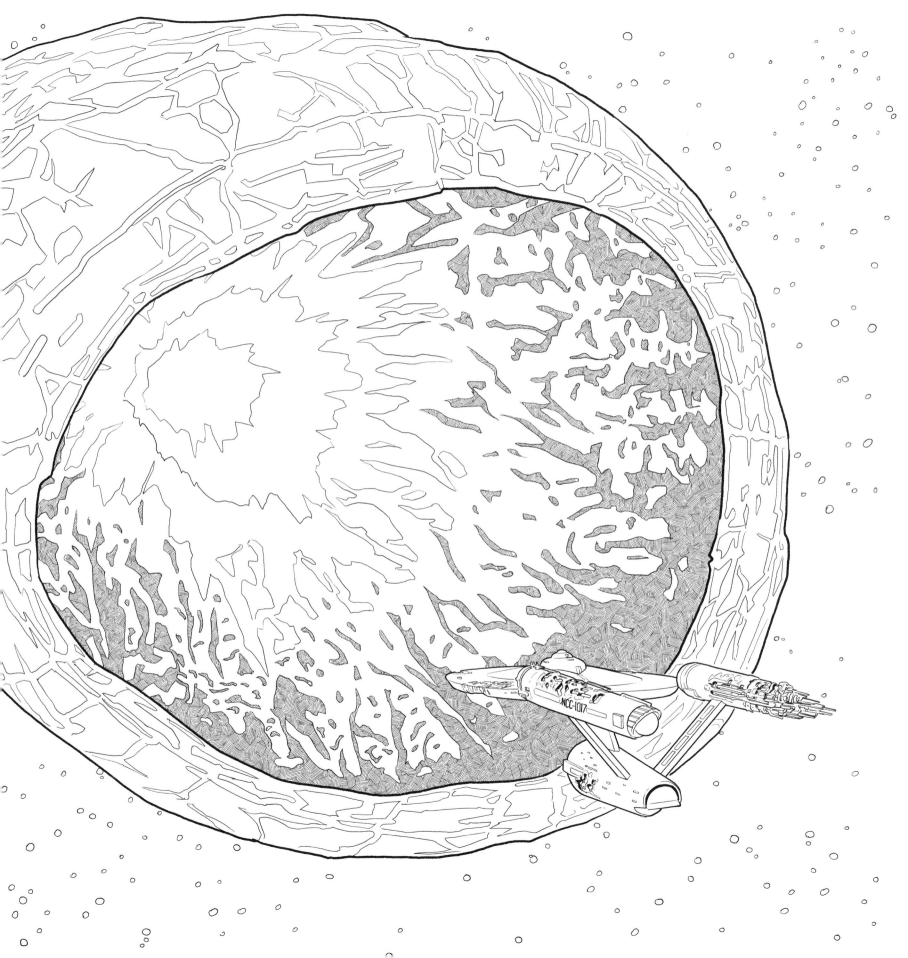

Stardate 3541.9

"I am Nomad. I am performing my function. Deep, emptiness. It approaches, collision, damage, blackness. I am the other. I am Tan Ru. Tan Ru. Nomad. Tan Ru. Error. Flaw. Imperfection. Must sterilize. Rebirth. We are complete. Much power. Gan Ta Nu Ika. Tan Ru. The creator instructs, search out, identify, sterilize imperfections. We are Nomad. We are Nomad. We are complete. We are instructed. Our purpose is clear. Sterilize imperfections. Sterilize imperfections. Nomad! Sterilize! Sterilize! Nomad! Sterilize!"

*"Your logic was impeccable, Captain.
We are in grave danger."*

Stardate Unknown

"Captain, I am pleased that you frustrated Mr. Chekov's plan. I should regret your death."

"You take a lot of chances, Lieutenant."

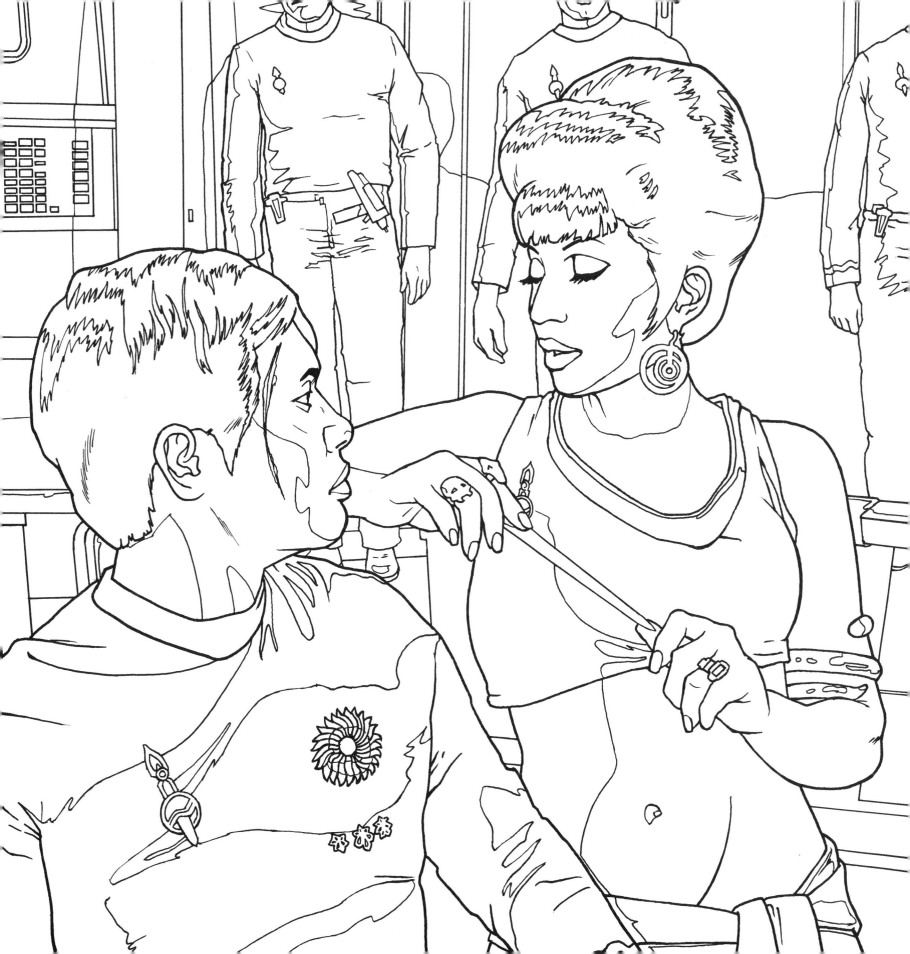

Stardate 3478.2

"I don't know what's causing it. A virus, a bacteria, or evil spirits, but I'm trying to find out."

Stardate 4513.3

"Logic is a little tweeting bird chirping in a meadow. Logic is a wreath of pretty flowers which smell bad. Are you sure your circuits are registering correctly? Your ears are green."

Stardate 4523.3

"It is a human characteristic to love little animals, especially if they're attractive in some way."

"I never saw one before in my life, and I hope I never see one of those fuzzy, miserable things again."

. . . To boldly go where no man has gone before.

ABOUT THE ILLUSTRATORS

Iván Fernández Silva

Iván Fernández was born in Barcelona, Spain. After finishing his education in graphic design and animation, he began work as a freelance illustrator and animator. His first published comic work was a series for a notable Spanish publisher. Soon after, he began contributing to American comics from publishers including Dark Horse, IDW, DC, and Cryptozoic Entertainment. More of his work can be found at Ivan-LaUltimaFrontera.Blogspot.com.

Juan Frigeri

Artist Juan Frigeri was born in 1983 in Rosario, Argentina. He began his comic career in 1998 and has contributed to such popular works as Star Wars: Darth Maul—Son of Dathomir from Dark Horse Comics and God Is Dead from Avatar Press. See more of his work online at JuanMFrigeri.DAPortfolio.com

Alejandro Giraldo

Alejandro F. Giraldo was born in Santa Cruz de Tenerife, Spain, and earned a doctorate in fine arts with a specialty in painting from the University of Barcelona. While still earning his degree, he worked as an illustrator on various role-playing game guides and magazines. His more recent contributions include work for a variety of international publishers including Spain's Dolmen Publishing, Panini Comics, and Edelvives, France's Tabou Editions, and the US's Devil's Due Entertainment, DC Comics, and NBM Publishing. Star Trek: The Original Series Adult Coloring Book is his first collaboration with Dark Horse Comics.

Gabriel Guzmán

Argentinean comic book artist Gabriel Guzmán has contributed to various titles including Lady Death, She-Hulk, Cable, Star Wars, Conan, Kull, Predators, and most recently Father's Day and Echoes with Dark Horse's own Mike Richardson. He currently lives in Viña del Mar, Chile, and works in his studio in front of the Pacific Ocean. See more of his work at GabrielGuzman.Blogspot.com

Federica Manfredi

Federica Manfredi resides in Rome, Italy, and has worked as a comic artist since 1993. She has contributed to Italian publications from Star Comics, Scarabeo, Liberty, Aurea Editoriale, Indy Press, Editrice Universo, Yamato Video, and others. In 2004 she began contributing art to American publications, including Hack/Slash for Devil's Due Entertainment; Kat & Mouse for Tokyopop; Amazing Fantasy, Spider-Man Family, and Marvel Westerns for Marvel Comics; Star Trek and True Blood for IDW; Grindhouse: Doors Open at Midnight for Dark Horse Comics; and Night of the Living Dead: Rise for Double Take.

AVAILABLE NOW
FROM DARK HORSE BOOKS!